HAZEL
tree
farm

one STORMY NIGHT

I am a reader

and I celebrated World Book Day 2023

with this gift from my local bookseller

and The O'Brien Press

WORLD BOOK DAY®

World Book Day's mission is to offer every child and young person the opportunity to read and love books by giving you the chance to have a book of your own.

To find out more, and for fun activities including the monthly World Book Day Book Club, video stories and book recommendations, **visit worldbookday.com**

World Book Day is a charity sponsored by National Book Tokens.

Alma Jordan lives on a farm in County Meath with her husband Mark and son Eamon. After a successful career in marketing and communications, she founded the award-winning social enterprise AgriKids in 2015 to spread the message of farm safety to children in a fun and engaging way.

Alma grew up on a farm in County Kildare, and the Hazel Tree Farm series features lots of real-life stories from her childhood, as well as moments shared by the children she meets through her work today.

HAZEL
tree
farm

one
STORMY
NIGHT

ALMA JORDAN

THE O'BRIEN PRESS
DUBLIN

First published 2023 by
The O'Brien Press Ltd,
12 Terenure Road East, Rathgar, Dublin 6, D06 HD27, Ireland.
Tel: +353 1 4923333; Fax: +353 1 4922777
E-mail: books@obrien.ie; Website: obrien.ie
The O'Brien Press is a member of Publishing Ireland.

ISBN: 978-1-78849-412-0

Design and layout by Emma Byrne.
Cover illustration by Margaret Anne Suggs.

1 3 5 7 8 6 4 2
23 25 27 26 24

Printed and bound in Great Britain by Clays Ltd, Elcograf S.p.A.

The paper in this book is produced using pulp from managed forests.

Time passed by, and more trees grew
Bigger and stronger — that may be true.
But no tree stood with more magic and charm
Than the hazel tree of Hazel Tree Farm.

Chapter 1

Chipper Chips

There is something special about the village of Ballynoe. It isn't the biggest village, nor is it the smallest, but it's definitely the friendliest and kindest. It's the sort of place where people say, 'Hello, how are you?' and actually mean it.

That's because the people of Ballynoe look out for one another. They are always there to lend a helping hand to a neighbour in need. Like when Mrs Kelly's cat didn't come home for tea. Or when the school needed a new roof, and everyone raised the money by holding a talent show. In fact, 'Ballynoe's Next Big Star' was such a success that not only did the school get a new roof but there was enough money left over for new goalposts and basketball hoops for the school yard too.(Although some people still believe Garda Liam playing the bodhrán should have been the winner, not Sally Williams's singing budgie.)

If you travel beyond the bridge of Ballynoe village, you will soon be surrounded by fields and woodland. To the untrained eye, such scenery all looks the same, and most people just keep on driving until they get to the next town. Which is a pity, as they miss out on the most amazing sounds you could ever hear.

Like the *Mooooooo Mooooooooo* of the cows waiting to be milked at Doyle Dairies.

Or the *Cluck Cluck Cluck, Cluck Cluck Cluck, Cockadoodle Doo* coming from Cooper's Chicken Farm.

And if you hear the *Baaaaaa Baaaaaaaa* of sheep, that can only mean one thing: you have arrived at Hazel Tree Farm.

Peter and Kate Farrelly live at Hazel Tree Farm, along with their Mam and Dad. They love nothing more than waking up to the sounds and smells – even the yucky ones! – of farm life.

In case you are wondering why it is called Hazel

Tree Farm (and that is a good thing to wonder), the answer lies in the woods behind the meadow. There stands the lone hazel tree, whose branches in the summer shade all who sit beneath it, and in the winter offer shelter from the wind and rain. In spring, newborn lambs run and play around its trunk in what Dad calls their 'evening frolics'.

The humans of Hazel Tree Farm had also left their mark on this tree over the years. Four generations of the Farrelly family climbed its branches and carved their initials into its bark. If they look close enough, Peter and Kate can still make out their great-great-grandad's name. The hazel tree, which everyone sees as a symbol of knowledge and wisdom, had witnessed many a happy day at Hazel Tree Farm.

Today, however, was not one of those days …

'Careful, Peter!' wailed Mam. 'That's very delicate! You too, Kate.' Mam turned her attention to her daughter, who was tugging a little too hard on a Christmas bauble. 'Oh, just let me do it.'

Mam had had enough. She rolled up her sleeves and took over the operations.

'I haaaaaate taking down the Christmas tree,'

11

grumbled Kate as Mam handed her each bauble, one by one. Kate wrapped them in bubble wrap before placing them carefully in the ancient cardboard box, all under Mam's watchful eye.

Kate's older brother Peter, however, was in one of his giddy moods.

'Whoo, steady, steady,' he said, jokingly swaying from side to side, balancing one of Mam's Christmas ornaments in his hand. 'Oh, my hands are sooooooo slippery and this Santa is soooo heavy …'

Mam froze. 'Peter, stop that immediately,' she commanded.

As if able to see what was coming, Kate closed her eyes just as the sound of smashing china rang out across the sitting room.

Peter stood perfectly still. Had that really just happened? He slowly looked down to see poor Santa and Rudolph in many pieces at his feet.

'Sorry, Mam,' he said awkwardly. 'I'll tidy it up.'

From the top step of the ladder, Mam looked down sadly. That ornament had been a present from their next-door neighbours, the Coopers, to mark Peter's first Christmas, nine years ago. She still remembered a baby Peter gurgling in his crib as she and Dad unwrapped it. That year and every year since, it had sat on the windowsill closest to Cooper's Farm. Now she watched as Peter collected its pieces with a dustpan and brush. The once jolly face of Santa was ruined, and Rudolph's red nose rolled around the floor as he chased it with his brush.

Mam sighed. It was always such an exciting day when they put up the Christmas decorations, but taking them down was another thing altogether.

'This has to be the saddest day of the year,' Kate moaned, as she unwrapped the tinsel from around the tree.

'Why can't it be Christmas for longer?' added Peter. He decided to stay away from the breakable Christmas ornaments and instead reached for a sprig of holly over the fireplace.

'Ouch!' he cried, pricking his finger on a thorny leaf. A little dot of blood appeared on his fingertip.

'Oh, Peter,' Mam said gently, forgetting she was still quite cross with him. 'Run your hand under some cold water.'

As Peter splashed and soothed the redness away, he

felt a bit sorry for himself. Only a few days ago, the house had been full of people laughing and having fun. Presents were never-ending, and for some strange reason it was perfectly ok for them to eat chocolate first thing in the morning. Now everything was going back to boring old normal, and on Monday, it was back to school.

YUCK!

'Have you two forgotten your Christmas spirit already?' laughed Mam as she stepped down the ladder. 'If it was Christmas every day, you would soon get tired of it, and then you would have nothing to look forward to.'

Wrapping a tissue around his sore finger, Peter nodded glumly while Kate wrapped the Christmas fairy in tissue paper and yet more bubble wrap.

The fairy had been so pretty at the top of their tree, overlooking the happy Christmas scenes. Her blue dress had sparkled with the twinkling of the lights and even though her smile was painted on, to Kate, it looked real.

'See you next year,' whispered Kate as she covered her small porcelain face and packed her away, making sure she was on top, where she belonged.

'Oh no, have I missed it?' Dad was standing at the door of the living room, still wearing his wellie boots and work coat. He couldn't keep the smile off his face.

Mam placed her hands on her hips and pretended to be cross. 'How very convenient,' she joked, 'arriving just as the last ornament has been packed away.'

'Dad, where were you?' exclaimed Kate.

'We could've used an extra pair of hands,' added Peter, showing Dad his bandaged finger.

'Oh, I hate taking down the decorations,' Dad said, making a face. 'It's so depressing.'

He started to remove his boots and coat, planning to sit down and rest after what had been a long day on the farm. Mam, however, had other ideas.

'No slackers here, David Farrelly,' she said, pushing the largest of the boxes in his direction. 'You're on attic duties.'

Dad plodded slowly upstairs, pulled down the ladder and carried the first box up to the attic. As he clicked the light switch, his eyes fell on the old cot and buggies that Kate and Peter had once used. Time seemed to move so slowly back then, he thought, and so quickly now.

'Come on, David, this one's heavy!' He was snapped out of his daydream by Mam's voice down below, as she struggled under the weight of the next box.

* * *

Back down in the kitchen, with the decorations packed away for another year, the children still felt glum. Mam put her arms around both their shoulders.

'I know what'll cheer us all up,' she said, smiling. 'Chipper chips for tea!'

Peter's eyes lit up. He absolutely *loved* chipper chips.

'Can I get a snack box, with extra chicken?' he asked, excitedly.

'Can I get curry sauce?' said Kate, jumping up and down.

'Can I have a quarter pounder with extra cheese?' added Dad.

'You can have what you like, because you're going to get them,' laughed Mam.

Dad's face fell. 'Oh, Marian, I've had such a hard

day,' he protested. 'I've been getting the sheep pens ready for lambing and bedding them down and setting up the heat lamps and loading ewes and …'

But it was no use – Mam wasn't listening. She had work to do as well and was already dressed in her scrubs. She headed towards her veterinary clinic, which was located at the back of the farmhouse. She had follow-up calls to make, including checking in on a sausage dog who had eaten too many sausages and a gerbil with the hiccups.

'Make mine a battered sausage, and don't forget extra salt and vinegar!' she called to Dad on her way out.

'What's this about a battered sausage?' asked their neighbour, Eamon Cooper, who was standing in their hallway. 'I tried knocking, but no one was around.'

The children grinned. 'We're having chipper chips for tea!' cried Peter.

'Ooooh, sounds lovely,' laughed Eamon, rubbing his belly.

Eamon and Maggie Cooper's chicken farm was right next door. Eamon was also a sheep farmer and helped Dad manage the flock at Hazel Tree Farm.

'You're more than welcome to join us,' said Dad.

Eamon put up his hands and shook his head. 'No, no, Maggie has tea waiting. I was hoping Marian could take a look at my Peg. She's not herself this evening.'

Peg was Eamon and Maggie's border collie and the apple of Eamon's eye. She was a whizz at herding sheep and guarding the hens. She was also a champion at sheep trials, and Eamon had the trophies and ribbons to prove it.

'Oh no,' said Dad. 'She seemed fine earlier on.'

Some of the ewes at Hazel Tree Farm were due to have their lambs in the next two weeks. Earlier that day, Dad and Eamon had hitched the trailer and moved them from their field to the lambing shed. As always, Peg was there to keep an eye on the job. She guided the ewes up the ramp of the trailer and didn't move until she was sure they were all in and the door was closed. Then she jumped into the passenger seat of the jeep, leaving Eamon to sit behind 'the boss'. Dad drove the short distance to the lambing shed, where the pens were ready with thick straw beds and plenty of fresh water.

But now, it seemed that Peg had taken a turn.

'It looks to be an upset tummy, and she's gone right off her food,' sighed Eamon. 'That's not like my Peg.'

'You wait there,' said Dad, heading in the direction of Mam's clinic. 'I'll get Marian.'

Eamon smiled. 'That would be great,' he said, relieved. 'I really hope I'm not bothering her.'

'Don't worry,' Kate chimed in. 'Whatever it is, Mam will know what to do.'

'Maybe she just ate something bad,' added Peter. 'Shep did that once, and he was right as rain after a few days.'

Eamon hadn't heard the children mention their old dog Shep in quite a while. Shep's passing the previous year had been very hard on Peter and Kate, and Eamon knew that Peg being ill would bring back painful memories for them. Even as Peter and Kate tried to reassure him, he could hear a note of worry in their voices too.

Shep had already been at Hazel Tree Farm for five years when Peter was born. He was a rescue dog, 'a cross between a Labrador and an angel' according to Eamon's wife Maggie. Mam and Dad wondered how he would react to a new baby in the house, but Shep immediately took Peter under his protective paw. He whimpered when Peter cried and stood patiently under his highchair in the hope that a tasty morsel would fall his way. His big-brother duties doubled when Kate arrived two years later, and he was often seen giving baby Kate a gentle lick or trotting around after Peter as he learned to walk.

No one could have predicted Shep's passing. He had been fine that morning, running after Dad's lawnmower, barking at the wheels. For an old dog, he was fit and had hardly been sick a day in his life. But by that evening, he couldn't get up. He just lay there, panting. Dad had tried to stand him up, but his legs wouldn't hold his weight and he struggled to catch a breath.

Mam listened to his heart, which was beating slowly, very slowly. His paws were cold to the touch, and Mam knew what that meant: Shep's heart was slowing down, and there was nothing she could do to get it to beat faster. 'He's not in pain,' she whispered to the children, trying to smile, 'but I will give him something to make him more comfortable.'

'But there's still a chance he'll be ok?' Peter pleaded.

'He's very unwell, love,' said Mam. 'I'm afraid there's nothing we can do but stay with him and make sure he doesn't suffer.'

Dad moved Shep to an armchair in the kitchen, and Peter laid his old baby blanket across him. It was Shep's favourite. It was really soft, covered in stars and clouds. 'There you go, boy,' he said, gently rubbing Shep's head.

Kate choked back tears as she sank her face into his fur. 'You are best dog in the world. I love you so much.'

Shep passed away later that night. His final memories were ones of love and a family that adored him. They buried him in their garden, choosing the spot where he sheltered on warm days, with the best view of all that was going on.

Eamon remembered his wife Maggie telling the children to always talk about Shep, and that way, he was never really gone. As always, she was right; time had healed the wounds left by Shep's passing, yet his memory remained.

'Hello, Eamon. What's this about Peg?' Mam said

as she arrived in the hallway, her face concerned.

Eamon explained how Peg had eaten a little bit of food but had been quite sick, and now she was just lying down in front of the stove.

'Do you think she may have eaten something poisonous?' asked Eamon. He remembered that they had put bait boxes down to get rid of rodents – maybe she accidentally ate some of the poison?

As Mam was asking Eamon more about Peg's symptoms, his phone rang loudly, giving them all a fright. 'It's Maggie,' he said, answering it.

The children could hear Maggie's excited voice on the other end, telling Eamon that Peg was now sitting up and looking a bit brighter. Eamon let out an audible sigh of relief and nodded to Mam, who was smiling broadly.

'That sounds better,' she said. 'But keep her on a bland diet of porridge and rice for the next twenty-four hours, and if you're still worried tomorrow, bring her in to me.'

The children watched Eamon leave, thrilled that Peg was doing better and excited for their supper of chipper chips.

Chapter 2

Surprise Visitors

'Peter! Kate!' Mam called as loudly as she could. It was the first day back to school after the Christmas holidays, and even though the children had been called three times, there was still neither sight nor sound of them.

'Arrrrrgh!' groaned Peter, pulling the edges of his pillow over his ears. 'I'm just putting on my socks,' he lied.

'Coming, Mam!' Kate called out as she rinsed and spat the toothpaste down the sink. She pushed open the door of Peter's room. 'Come on, lazy bones. You're only making it worse.'

'It's toooo earlyyyyyyyyyyyyyy!' Peter snapped

back. 'Go away!'

Suddenly Peter felt something grab his feet, and his whole body started sliding down the length of the bed. He landed in a heap on his bedroom floor.

'Hey!' he exclaimed angrily. 'What did you do that for?'

Kate rubbed her hands together and giggled, feeling very proud of herself. Despite being younger and a little smaller than Peter, she was very strong for seven and a half.

'Eh, you're welcome,' she said triumphantly. 'Now you're really up!' She strode out of the room, leaving her brother sulking at the foot of his bed.

Peter threw back his curtains, still in a grump, and saw that it was a glorious morning at Hazel Tree Farm. He couldn't help but smile. The sheep were in the meadow, enjoying some rare January sunshine. His dad would soon bring more of them indoors to have their lambs, then the meadow would be full of new life and spring would officially begin.

Wish I was a sheep, thought Peter enviously.

'Peeeterrrrrrrr!' His mother's exasperated tone brought him back to reality.

'Nearly ready!' he replied as he reached for his school uniform. This time, it was almost true.

* * *

'*And now it's over to Marcus for the weather,*' the TV announcer said in a cheery tone, which was matched by the bouncy energy of the weather presenter.

'How can they be so chirpy at this hour of the morning?' groaned Peter, slumped in his chair at the kitchen table.

'They are sooooo annoying,' agreed Kate, as she plopped a lump of butter on her toast, watching a buttery puddle form before her eyes.

'Shhhh!' hissed Dad, glaring over at them.

Kate and Peter knew that tone. In fact, anyone who knows anything about farmers knows never to talk when the weather forecast is on. There could be a circus in the front room, with acrobats, clowns and parading ponies, but as soon as the weather map appears on the TV screen, everyone must be silent.

Farmers rely on the weather to help their crops grow and keep their animals safe. Some rain and some sun at the right time are vital, and even the wind is necessary to help dry and wilt grass for silage or hay. If it's too stormy or wet, the animals will need shelter and extra food.

'Can you turn that up, Marian?' Dad didn't take his eyes off the screen as he gestured to Mam.

Picking up the remote (which was closer to Dad, by the way), Mam turned up the sound. The sudden volume change made the children jump.

'Intermittent sunshine and unseasonably mild weather is forecast for the week ahead.' Marcus grinned from the TV screen, proudly showing the map behind him, which was dotted with pictures of suns and clouds. *'But don't go dusting off the sunscreen just yet …'*

Dad sat up in his chair.

'A low pressure moving in from the Atlantic may bring windier conditions across western parts of the country. Some light rain is also expected, with the chance of heavier showers in the east and north-east regions. So, for those children heading back to school today, I hope Santa brought you an umbrella and wellies – you might be needing them! Back to you in the studio, Teresa.'

Marcus's grinning face disappeared from the screen as Teresa moved on to a segment about getting fit after Christmas.

'Better check the sheds in the yard,' said Dad, standing up. 'I don't want any parts blowing in the wind or getting carried away.'

'Sure, you know the weather,' Mam said, trying to ease Dad's worry, 'it nearly always changes.'

But Dad wasn't listening. He was too busy making plans and thinking out loud. 'Will clean out the far shed and bed it down … Maybe bring in the other pregnant ewes a little sooner. I don't want them out in gale-force winds.'

'Who said anything about gale-force winds?' Mam rolled her eyes, but Dad was already halfway out the door.

She turned back to Peter and Kate and shook her head. 'Come on, you two. Unlike the weather, the school bus is a sure thing, and it won't wait.'

Belting down the rest of their breakfasts, Peter and Kate put on their coats and grabbed their schoolbags. Hugging their mother goodbye, they ran to the gate, just as the school bus appeared in the distance.

In the newly quiet kitchen, Mam filled the sink with sudsy water. Through the window, she could see Dad and Eamon examining the sides of the sheds. They tugged and pulled at the metal sheets and scratched their heads. Eamon was tapping his chin as Dad moved up and down, looking for any gaps or loose areas.

Mam had a rare day off today and was happy to have the house to herself. Once the cleaning was done, she was planning to bring their Christmas tree to the recycling centre for Ballynoe's 'Bring Your Tree for Free'. Every year, old trees were chopped up into mulch and used to decorate the gardens in Ballynoe Village Park.

Mam and Dad had already put the tree into the small trailer, which was hitched to the back of Mam's car. Before getting in, she checked that it was secure, that the knots were tight and not even a bump in the road could budge it. She sat into the front seat, and as she adjusted her mirrors, something suddenly caught her eye.

'What was that?' she whispered to herself, alarmed. She was sure she had seen something scurry around the corner of the house. Slowly opening the car door, Mam gingerly walked to the side of the house.

Oh, please don't be a rat, she thought, grimacing. Mam might have been a vet who cared for all animals, but she really hated rats. As she rounded the corner to the back of the house, she glanced left and right. Everything looked fine, nothing out of place. Then suddenly, out of nowhere, two chickens ran across her path.

'Ahhhhhhhhh!' screamed Mam, putting her hand on her chest. 'Get out of there!' The cheeky duo ran under the hedge and back to Cooper's Farm where they belonged.

Finding her breath once more, Mam realised where they had come from: the bike shed in their back yard. Some of the wood on the door had rotted away, leaving a large gap, plenty big enough for some naughty hens to wiggle through. The shed was used to store the children's bikes and scooters as well as the old lawnmower that, despite not working for many years, was still there, taking up space. Opening the door fully, Mam stepped inside, wanting to make sure there were no more feathery guests hiding.

CCCRRRRRAAAAAACCCCKKKKK!

'Ugh,' sighed Mam, looking down at the broken egg underfoot. It seemed that this was not the first time the hens had come. Mam went outside to clean her shoe on the grass. It was then that she spotted another animal, this time sniffing around her car – Benji the border collie, who belonged to their rather grumpy neighbour Mattie Kennedy.

The only time Mattie had spoken to Mam was when he brought Benji to her surgery with a sore paw. He liked to keep to himself – he didn't have family of his own and wasn't someone who enjoyed visitors.

During a very bad snowstorm, Dad had offered to clear his blocked driveway with the tractor and bucket.

'Leave it be,' Mattie had snapped. 'It'll melt when its ready.'

His home was somewhat neglected. The rusted gate hung to one side, and the paint was peeling from the walls of the main house. Some of the curtains were always drawn, and in the summer, you couldn't see the front door as the grass grew so high.

Mattie may not have taken care of his house, but the same couldn't be said about Benji, who was a fine, strong dog with a gleaming coat. He had three black paws and one that was white with black speckles. He sat up as Mam approached, offering her his speckled paw.

'You are a good boy,' said Mam gently, 'but you shouldn't be here. I'm sure your master is looking for you.'

At that moment, she heard a loud call. 'BENJI! BENJI!' Mattie Kennedy was coming up the road towards Hazel Tree Farm, his walking stick tapping with each stride. He stopped at the Farrellys' gate to take a breath, leaning on his walking stick as he did so.

Benji turned and headed towards his master, with Mam following him. 'He's here, Mattie!' she called to her neighbour.

Mattie swung in Mam's direction, his face darkening with rage. 'You need to keep your gates closed. My dog could've been lost in your fields.'

Taken aback, Mam folded her arms in annoyance. 'It's best to keep your own gates closed, Mattie,' she said abruptly. 'We'll be lambing soon, and a loose dog

31

can upset and hurt the ewes and lambs.'

Without saying another word, Mattie turned crossly and headed for home. Benji walked behind his master, head lowered, knowing he was in trouble.

Hmmmm, thought Mam. *I really hope that's the last we see of Benji up here. That man is so rude.*

Back in the yard, another border collie, Peg, was the main topic of conversation between Dad and Eamon.

'She seemed better this morning,' said Eamon as he tightened the screws on the shed door. 'She even finished most of her porridge.'

'Where is she now?' asked Dad, thinking it was strange not to see Peg at Eamon's side.

'On a blanket in front of the stove,' said Eamon, smiling. 'Maggie wants to keep an eye on her.'

Chapter 3

Greedy Chicks

'Cluck cluck cluck!' called Maggie as a flutter of feathery beings ran towards her.

The sight of her hens first thing in the morning always made her smile. They reminded her of when she was a little girl growing up in the Caribbean. Her family had a small farm with some cows and goats. They used their milk to make butter and cheese to sell at local markets. As soon as she was old enough, Maggie took her pocket money and bought some hens. The money she earned selling their eggs was used to pay for more hens, which gave her more eggs to sell.

She developed such a love for these funny little

creatures that she jumped at the chance to study agriculture in Ireland and to work on an Irish chicken farm. Little did she realise when she arrived as a shy young woman to Cooper's Chicken Farm all those years ago that she would fall in love with Eamon, stay forever and live a life she could only have dreamed of.

The Coopers had one large hen house, which was also home to a rooster called Rodney. There were some smaller sheds too, used to store the chickens' food and bedding as well as tools and some machinery.

Maggie opened up a small shed and peeked inside. A few weeks ago, one of their hens was caught in the bike shed at Hazel Tree Farm. She was probably looking around for a safe place to hatch her chicks, and in the end, she chose this spot instead. The seven little furballs now scampered after their mother, staying as close as they could. The yard was a big and scary place for a week-old chick!

'Hey you, stop that,' Maggie laughed as one of the chicks pecked at her shoe. This chick was much braver than its siblings. It wasn't afraid to break away from the brood and explore other areas of the yard. Its protective mother would come scampering after it, wings aloft and feathers puffed out, pushing it back to join the others. But it wouldn't be long before this little rogue was heading off again.

Hearing footsteps, Maggie looked up to see Mam and Kate coming towards her.

'Good morning, my lovelies,' she exclaimed. 'Have you come to see my chicks?'

'I can't keep Kate away,' laughed Mam, as Kate ran towards Maggie, scattering the chicks in all directions. If anyone loved hens as much as Maggie, it was Kate.

'Slow down there,' laughed Maggie. 'Let them come to you, but you must stand perfectly still.'

Listening to her wise words, Kate stood as still as a statue. Maggie scattered some feed at Kate's feet and watched as the Mama Hen came forward and pecked at it. Confident that there was no danger, her chicks quickly followed.

Kate squealed (quietly) at the sight and sound of the little ones. 'They are the most adorable things I have ever seen,' she sighed.

Tap Tap Tap

The little rogue chick was pecking at Kate's shoe. Its soft down was yellow and fluffy, just what a young chick needed to keep it warm. Kate crouched slowly, hoping the chick wouldn't scarper, but instead it hopped onto her other shoe.

Tap Tap Tap

Kate giggled.

'Put your hand out, Kate,' whispered Maggie. She poured some of the chicken crumb onto Kate's out-stretched hand and pointed downwards.

Following Maggie's directions, Kate lowered her hand to the ground.

At first the chick didn't move, unsure of this strange situation. But the promise of some delicious crumb enticed it to hop closer. A little peck at Kate's finger-tips and then it gingerly hopped onto the curved area between her thumb and fingers. It looked up at Kate, cocking its head and chirping.

Kate didn't dare take a breath.

'Go on, little chick, go on,' Maggie whispered.

With one sudden movement, the little chick hopped into Kate's palm and pecked at the crumb. Kate's mouth fell open in amazement. 'What do I do next?' she whispered to Maggie, her eyes wide as saucers.

'Cup your two hands together,' said Maggie. 'That way, it won't fall. Their little bones are so fragile, we must be careful how we handle these babies.'

With her hands cupped, Kate smiled as the little chick ate its fill. Mam, meanwhile, kept an eye out for Mama Hen. She might not be too happy to see her young chick so far away and in the hands of a human, even one as gentle as Kate.

Maggie noticed the special bond forming between Kate and this little chick. It was something she too had experienced with her first hen as a child, and this made her very happy.

Once all the hens had been fed, Mam, Kate and Maggie headed up to Cooper's Cottage for a cup of tea and a slice of Maggie's apple tart. Maggie was an amazing baker, and there was always a delicious treat (or two) for visitors.

Eamon and Peg were already there. Eamon was poking at the fire, while Peg snoozed in front of it.

As she watched the sleeping dog, Mam was reminded of her quarrel with Mattie Kennedy a few weeks ago. Even though Benji had not returned – at least not that she knew of – she had been troubled by it. She had never seen Benji wander the roads like that before. Was there something pulling him away from his home? She really hoped it wasn't the sheep drawing him – that could be a disaster.

'Penny for your thoughts,' Eamon said, smiling.

'What's a penny?' asked Kate through a mouthful of cookie that Maggie had snuck to her.

Mam told the Coopers about her run-in with Benji and Mattie.

'He's a fine dog, that Benji,' mused Eamon. 'I often thought he and my Peg would have a good litter of pups.'

'But no dog was ever good enough for his Benji,' Maggie said, rolling her eyes.

'Oh, puppies would be the best,' cried Kate. 'Peg would be a lovely mummy.'

'How is Peg?' Mam asked, studying the sleeping dog once more.

'Well, I'm glad you asked,' laughed Eamon. 'She bounced back after that tummy bug earlier in the month, but she does seem tired lately. Might be her age. She's not the young one she used to be.'

'Happens to the best of us!' Maggie called from the sink as she filled the kettle.

'Is she eating ok?' Mam continued.

'Well, if I'm to be honest, she seems up and down,' admitted Eamon. 'Her appetite is all over the place. Do you think it could be something else, Marian?'

'I can't be sure,' Mam said, 'but I would like you to bring Peg to the surgery later. I can do a proper scan.'

'A scan,' echoed Maggie, moving towards them.

Eamon looked very worried. 'What's wrong with her?'

'I believe there is absolutely nothing wrong with her,' laughed Mam, confusing everyone. 'After I scan her, we'll know more.'

Kate sat down at Peg's side, gently rubbing her back. She didn't look sick. In fact, her rounded tummy and glossy coat made her look very healthy. Kate tuned out the grownups and let her mind wander to the little chick she had held earlier. It was so cute, and there was something special about the way it looked at her …

* * *

That evening, a reluctant Peg followed Mam and Eamon to the surgery. With sad eyes, she watched as Mam set up her scanning equipment. Eamon lifted her up and placed her gently on Mam's examination table. He took off his cap and rubbed the perspiration from his brow.

Mam squeezed a large dollop of clear gel onto her hand and rubbed it on Peg's stomach. She pulled a TV monitor in between her and Eamon, so they both had a good view. She placed the round end of the hand-held scanner onto Peg's tummy, moving it in gentle circles. The screen flickered and Eamon, squinting at first, began to make out the pictures that were appearing in front of them.

Five little circles appeared on the screen, white on the outside and black in the middle, with a small bean-shaped outline. Each outline fluttered. A big smile spread across Mam's face. Her suspicions were right: by the looks of it, Peg had five puppies growing inside her.

'Well, I never,' gasped Eamon, blinking at the screen.

Pressing some buttons on her scanner, Mam measured the little circles and smiled at Eamon. 'According to the size of these sacs, Peg is about four weeks pregnant, nearly halfway.'

Eamon was in shock. How had he missed this?

'Don't you worry, Peg,' he said, giving her a gentle pat, 'we'll take great care of you and your family.'

In the kitchen, Maggie, Dad, Peter and Kate were all waiting for news. As Mam and Eamon entered with Peg, Eamon held up his hand, showing all five fingers.

'Five puppies,' he said. 'Our Peg is going to be a mum.'

Dad put his arm around a stunned Maggie, who began to shake and sob.

Peter turned to Kate. 'You know what this means?'

Kate's eyes grew huge. 'PUPPIES,' she squealed, 'we're going to have puppies!'

'Is there any way of telling who the sire is or what their breed is?' Eamon asked Mam, suddenly looking worried. Peg was a champion sheepdog, and given the choice, he would have picked another champ to father her puppies.

'Not at this stage,' answered Mam. 'We'll just have

to wait and see. I believe Peg will be due her puppies at the beginning of March.'

With a big yawn and a stretch, Peg found the armchair in the corner of the kitchen and crawled up into it. Normally she would be in the middle of all this excitement, barking and playing, but not today. Today she felt too tired. As the noises from the humans faded into the background, Peg closed her eyes and snoozed.

Chapter 4

A Storm Is Brewing

Despite the weather forecast, January had been mild and dry. Dad and Eamon couldn't be happier, as the first of the lambs were thriving and already outdoors with their mums.

By Valentine's Day, lambing season was in full swing. It would soon be time to move the next batch of pregnant ewes indoors in preparation for their big day.

'Flowers for you, my love.' Eamon bowed and presented Maggie with a bunch of roses and box of Valentine's chocolates.

Maggie giggled. 'You old softie,' she said, as she pecked her husband on the cheek and reached into the pocket of her apron for a heart-shaped cookie, wrapped in a ribbon.

'No one can bake like you, Maggie Cooper,' grinned Eamon, taking a big bite.

The arrival of March meant that Peg's puppies were soon due. She had grown weary and now spent most of her time sleeping and eating.

When it came to animals giving birth, Maggie only knew about chickens and sheep, so she had asked Mam for her help in getting everything set up for the new arrivals. In front of the stove was Peg's whelping box, where she would deliver her puppies. This was Peg's favourite place to lie, and Maggie wanted to keep things familiar and quiet for her. It was also important that the puppies were kept warm when they were delivered, or they might not survive.

Eamon was relieved that Mam was next door. At eight years old, Peg was still very active on the farm, but she was considered quite old to be having puppies. She was healthy, though, and so far everything was going perfectly. Still, having a skilled vet like Marian Farrelly close by gave him peace of mind.

As some farm babies were due to be born, others

were growing up fast. Maggie's once fluffy chicks were now getting feathers of their own. The little one that Kate had cradled at just a week old was turning cream with brown speckles. It was still cheeky and inquisitive and followed Kate whenever she visited the Coopers' yard.

Kate loved weekend mornings, when she came over to help Maggie take care of the hens. Not many seven-year-olds would enjoy mucking out and bedding down, but Kate wasn't your typical seven-year-old. Maggie could see she was a natural with all animals, but she had a special connection when it came to the chickens.

'Watch it, Kate,' laughed Maggie one March morning. 'Your number-one fan is at your feet again!'

Kate laughed as the chick chirped up at her, waiting for her to scoop it up. Maggie saw how careful Kate was with the chick, and she knew it was time for a reward.

'I was thinking,' she began, 'that it's time to find that little hen a new home.'

'Why?' cried Kate. 'Has she done something wrong?'

'Well, I think she would be happier living somewhere else,' continued Maggie. 'Somewhere like, I don't know, Hazel Tree Farm, perhaps?'

Kate shot a look to Maggie. 'What are you saying?' she asked, knowing the answer but not daring to believe it.

'I think it's about time you had a hen of your own.' Maggie put down her sweeping brush and stood beside the stunned little girl. 'You have a natural way with animals, Kate, and I think they like you too.'

'Oh, I'll take the bestest care of her!' Kate's voice croaked with emotion. 'She will have the softest bed, the tastiest grain and the freshest water.'

Maggie laughed. 'I have no doubt! Now what will you call her?'

From the first time she held her, Kate had always referred to her as 'little chick'. But she wasn't going to be little or a chick for much longer. She frowned, and then a great idea came to her. 'There's a character in my favourite book called Henrietta Patterson. She's a hen detective and is super smart.'

'That's a fine name,' said Maggie. 'Do you know what's short for Henrietta?'

Kate's eyes grew huge, and a smile spread across her face. 'Hettie!' she squealed, then turned to her new chick. 'I am going to call you Hettie!'

Maggie nodded her head in approval. 'Now let's put these little ones in,' she said. 'I don't like the look of that sky.'

Back when Maggie was a child, her father would predict the weather not by listening to the news but by looking at the sky or watching how the animals were behaving. If his cattle grouped together and became restless or if birds were flying low, he knew a storm was brewing.

'Red sky at night, the shepherd's delight,' she rhymed, as Kate looked up. 'Red sky in the morning is a shepherd's warning.'

* * *

Over in the Coopers' kitchen, Dad, Eamon and Peter were having a well-earned cuppa after what had been a busy night in the lambing shed. Peter was feeling pretty chuffed with himself and a proper part of the team.

He had woken early that morning and ran

straight to the shed once he saw the lights were on. When he arrived, Dad and Eamon said they had everything under control, but Peter noticed that one ewe seemed to be in difficulty. Her lamb was being delivered head-first, with no sign of its two front feet, which meant they were still inside the ewe. Peter knew this wasn't right and called Eamon over.

'It's hung, Peter,' said Eamon. He looked over to Dad, but he was busy pulling another lamb. 'Right, it's up to us. Grab a bucket of water and keep the head wet. We can't let it swell, or we're in real trouble.'

Peter understood the seriousness of the situation. He put on the long gloves that Eamon handed him and began to lightly wet the lamb's head.

Eamon moved the ewe onto her side to make her more comfortable. 'We'll have to push the lamb's head back and then find the two front feet.'

But it was a big lamb, and the head was large, making the job difficult. Eamon had to try something else. Not wanting to cause the ewe more stress, he tried to locate the feet by sliding his hand alongside the neck of the lamb and inside the ewe.

The ewe was panting heavily so Peter moved to

the front and placed his hand on her back, hoping it would soothe her. 'Good girl,' he whispered gently. 'You'll have your lamb soon.'

'Hey, hey,' laughed Eamon suddenly, 'I found a leg!' Eamon pushed in deeper, moving the leg forward so that a small hoof emerged alongside the head. It wasn't a perfect situation, but it was better. He repeated the process on the other side.

With great skill and to Peter's delight, Eamon safely brought the lamb into the world. As it landed on the straw bed, Eamon set to work to help it breathe. He rubbed the lamb's tiny chest and then lifted its head. He put his fingers into its mouth, clearing out any mucus he found. Picking it up by its back legs, he gently swung it forward and back to release more fluid. He checked its airways once more. Shaking his head, he started to rub its back and chest again.

Peter reached out and grabbed a piece of the straw bedding. Using the straw, he tickled each of the lamb's nostrils. Suddenly, a tiny sneeze could be heard, and the lamb shook its head.

'That's it, Peter!' said Eamon happily. 'Those are

shepherd's instincts you have.'

With Eamon's permission, Peter moved the lamb beside its mother so that she could lick it clean and start forming a bond. A short while later, it was standing on its own and taking its first drink.

'What a night,' said Dad now, cradling the warm cup of tea in his hands and smiling across the kitchen table at his son.

'It sure was,' agreed Peter.

'That's nearly half the lambs born safely,' said Eamon, taking a mouthful of tea. 'Hopefully it'll be quieter today and we can all get some rest.'

From her place in front of the stove, Peg wagged her tail as the humans talked. It was as if she understood every word and wanted to be part of their conversation, especially one that involved sheep.

'And now the weather.'

The radio crackled in the corner as Kate and Maggie came into the kitchen.

'*SHHHHHHHH!*' was Dad and Eamon's collective greeting. Maggie and Kate just smiled and rolled their eyes.

'The Met Office has issued an amber weather alert for

much of the country from 5pm today. Strong gales origi-nally forecast for Monday will land earlier than expected. No unnecessary journeys should be taken, especially along coastal routes in the west and southwest. Stay tuned for updates. But for now, it's back to you in the studio.'

'It's all this mild weather we've been having,' said Dad, shaking his head. 'It's brewing up a storm.'

'Thankfully we have those loose sheets taken care of,' said Eamon.

'Peter, we can throw in extra feed and bedding to keep the ewes and lambs warm and settled through the night,' added Dad. 'Once the storm hits this even-ing, we'll all need to stay inside.'

'While you all make your plans, I'll walk Kate back home,' said Maggie. 'We can check out where Hettie will live.'

'Will it be a bad storm?' Kate asked, feeling uneasy since she heard the weather forecast.

Maggie took her hand and squeezed it tight. 'We'll all be fine once we're indoors,' she said with a smile.

As the humans left to prepare for the storm, Peg sniffed the air and let out a whimper. She could sense danger, and her protective instincts went on high alert. She could feel the life inside her. With ears now pricked, she sat up, suddenly not feeling tired anymore.

Chapter 5

Peg Goes Missing

By five o'clock, the sky was dark and there was a stillness in the air that made Eamon uneasy. *The storm is coming in*, he thought to himself. *Right on time too.*

He decided to check on the animals one more time. The hens were gently cackling, and some were perched on their roosts, their heads lowered, sleeping soundly.

'Good girls,' said Eamon, relieved. Rodney was pecking around on the ground, busy but settled. Giving the doors an extra tug, Eamon headed for home.

In Cooper's Cottage, Maggie was tending to a restless Peg, who wouldn't stop walking around the kitchen.

'Do you need to do your business?' asked Maggie, opening the back door. Peg's ears pricked up. She bolted for the door and dashed past a stunned Maggie.

'Peg!' she cried in horror. 'Come back!'

❋ ❋ ❋

Next door at Hazel Tree Farm, a cosy Sunday evening was on the cards. The smell of spaghetti bolognese filled the kitchen, everyone's favourite dinner.

'Did you wash your hands?' Mam called out to the children.

'No,' they chorused and slumped to the bathroom.

Dad came in the back door. Like Eamon, he had been checking on the animals. Three more ewes had lambed, and he was confident that no more lambs would be born that night.

'It's getting wild out there,' he said to Mam as he took off his boots and hung up his work coat. The lights flickered.

'That's spooky,' said Kate, coming back into the kitchen.

'Woooooo wooooooo!' wailed Peter, throwing up his hands like a ghost.

'Mam!' cried Kate. 'Peter's scaring me.'

'Stop scaring your sister, Peter,' said Mam as she stirred the spaghetti in the boiling water.

Dad went to the DIY drawer and took out two torches and an extra set of batteries. 'Just in case the electricity goes.'

As the family sat down to dinner, the storm had landed and the wind outside howled. It whistled through the trees and rattled the farmyard gates. The driving rain danced off the windows of the house and the metal rooftops of the farm sheds.

'How nice to be inside,' said Dad, as he twisted the pasta around his fork.

'Hmmmmm,' Peter hummed in agreement, slurping up a long strand of spaghetti.

'Yuck, Peter,' grumbled Kate, 'you're splattering tomato sauce all over your face.'

'Peter, clean your mouth,' said Mam, reaching behind her for a napkin. But as she turned back around, she caught him rubbing his sleeve across his face, leaving an orangey-red streak at the end of his sweatshirt.

'Peter …' Mam sighed in annoyance. She leaned

over to wipe his face properly, just as a loud knocking came at their back door.

'Who could that be?' asked Mam, alarmed.

Dad got up from the table and opened the door. Maggie and Eamon bundled inside, their raincoats dripping water all over the floor and their faces pale with worry.

'It's Peg,' cried Eamon. 'She's missing.'

'She wanted to go outside,' said Maggie, fighting back tears. 'I thought she wanted to go to the toilet, so I opened the door, and she just took off.'

Peter and Kate looked at Dad, their eyes wide with fear. Dad grabbed his coat and pulled on his boots.

'The weather is so bad,' said Mam. 'Be careful. I'm sure she's not too far away.'

'We've been calling her and calling her,' said Eamon, 'but there's no sign. We thought she would be back as soon as the weather took a turn for the worse.'

'She is so close to having her puppies,' added Maggie. 'She can't be out in this weather.'

Dad picked up one of the torches. Peter and Kate stood to go too, but he shook his head. 'You two stay here,' he said sternly.

'But Dad …' Peter protested, but it was no use. When Dad said no, he meant no.

'I have my phone if you need me,' Dad called back, slamming the door behind him as he left with Eamon and Maggie.

'Come on, you two, finish up your dinner,' Mam said, trying not to sound worried. 'I hope you left room for dessert.'

Outside, the wind was getting stronger. The children looked out the hall window and saw torch lights dancing in the distance. They could hear muffled voices calling, 'PEG! PEG!' Soon, though, the dancing light and the voices started to fade as the searchers went further into the night.

* * *

In the field behind the house stood the hazel tree of Hazel Tree Farm. The older residents of Ballynoe said it had been there for over a hundred years. On this night, it thrashed in the wind, its long, gnarled branches lifting and falling with the strong gusts that brushed against it.

Suddenly the might of the wind proved too much

for the old tree and it was pushed with astonishing strength, causing it to fall forward, the sound of its cracking trunk dimmed by the howling wind. As it fell, its upper branches became tangled with the electricity wires overhead. They whipped and snapped as the tree finally came crashing to the ground. Sparks flew from the electric pylons, lighting up the stormy sky for the briefest of moments.

* * *

Peter and Kate called out for Mam as the house was plunged into darkness.

'Don't worry,' she said, scrambling over to the torch Dad had left out. She switched it on and handed it to Peter.

'I should hold it,' said Kate, as she tried to grab the torch from Peter.

Peter held it over his head, out of his sister's reach. 'Here, take it!' he said mockingly.

'Stop it, you two,' their mother exclaimed. 'This is no time for squabbling.'

Mam turned on the torch app on her phone and rested it on the windowsill. Its light filled the darkened room. 'We're safe in here,' she said with a smile. 'We have light, a nice warm fire, and we still have dessert to eat.'

As they scooped up their jelly and ice cream, the children began to feel better. The wind and rain outside seemed to be easing, and the deafening noise subsided.

'What was that?' Kate could have sworn she heard a low whining noise. She looked crossly over at her brother. 'Stop making that noise, Peter. I know you're just trying to scare me.'

'What noise?' asked Peter. 'I'm not doing anything.'

'Shhhh,' said Mam. 'I said no more bickering.'

They sat in silence, the wind still whistling but the rain now just a gentle patter. Suddenly, they all heard the whining noise, this time followed by a loud bang. It was coming from outside.

'Mam, what is that?' Kate asked.

Mam flashed the phone's light through the window, trying to see. 'It's the door of the bike shed,' she said, relieved. 'It's after swinging wide open. I'm sure that whining noise was the old hinges.'

Putting on her coat, she made for the back door.

'Where are you going?' asked Kate.

'I'm going to close it over,' Mam replied, pulling her beanie hat down over her ears. 'It'll blow away if we leave it.'

Not wanting to be left alone, the children followed, putting on their own coats and boots.

'You two stay here,' Mam said sternly.

But this time Peter was not taking no for an answer. 'We're all going together,' he announced, shining his torch light out the back door.

'Ok,' Mam sighed, 'but stay close.'

All around them, trees swayed and the wind howled across the fields. Their back yard was encircled by the walls of sheds and the side of the house. They stayed close to the walls, which offered some shelter from the storm.

When they were only a few steps away from the shed, Kate heard the whining once again – and also whimpering. Mam, hearing it too, put her finger to her lips. As they stepped through the open door of the shed, the whining and whimpering were joined by a rustling, which was coming from the far corner on the right-hand side.

'There's definitely something in here,' said Peter, trying to sound braver than he felt.

Mam signalled to Peter to lift his torch, and together they illuminated the back wall. Kate clutched the back of her mother's coat. The light bounced off the wall and filled the darkened spaces. It lit up the bottles and tins of paint and varnish that stood on the shelves. Nothing unusual, nothing out of place.

Suddenly Kate jumped. A pair of eyes, shining emerald green, were staring straight back at them.

Peter gasped, but not in fear. 'Peg. It's Peg!'

As if relieved to see her friends, Peg gave another whimper. But she was also panting heavily.

'Is she hurt?' exclaimed Peter.

Mam shook her head. 'Peter, Kate,' she said, 'Peg needs our help. She's having her puppies.'

Chapter 6

Shep's Blanket

Mam shone her phone torch along the floor of the shed, which was scattered with bikes, scooters and rolls of rope and baling twine. Peg was tucked behind the broken lawnmower, lying down on old dust sheets and sacks. Not the situation Maggie had planned for, but Mam knew they had to work with what they had.

'I can hear something else,' whispered Peter. He shone his torch to the side of Peg. In the shadows, they could make out movement – a lot of movement.

It was puppies: not one, not two …

'Three puppies!' squealed Kate.

Mam put her finger to her lips once more and

gestured to the children to keep their voices down. Calmly, she dialled Dad's number. The children could hear their father on the other line, sounding flustered and worried.

'The search is over,' Mam said in quiet tones. 'Peg is here.'

After Dad promised to come straight over, Mam clicked off her phone and turned to the children. 'Peter, I want you to go back to the house immediately. We need blankets and supplies from my surgery.'

She listed off the items slowly. Peter nodded his head at each one, making sure to save it to his memory. Peg needed these things for her puppies. He couldn't make any mistakes.

When he was gone, Mam handed her phone to Kate and instructed her to keep the light low so as not to dazzle poor Peg. She rolled the old lawnmower outside and closed over the shed door. She had to make this area warmer and quieter.

'That's better,' she said, as she gently moved closer to examine Peg.

Kate followed, being careful to keep the light steady as Mam got to work.

The third little puppy, a female, had just been born. Mam cleared mucus from its mouth and moved it to Peg's side, where her first two puppies were already suckling milk. Mam was sure to keep them all close together and close to Peg for warmth.

'Good girl, Peg,' said Mam. 'You've done so well.'

Back in the house, Peter set to work filling a bag with the medical supplies Mam needed: gloves, a thermometer, antiseptic spray, a weighing scales, a notepad and pen, and plenty of towels.

Before heading back out, Peter paused. *I know what else Peg could have*, he thought. He ran upstairs and burst into his room, swinging open his closet door. He shone his torch along the shelves and pulled out his old baby blanket, the one that had belonged to Shep. *He'd want Peg to have this*, Peter thought, smiling.

When he arrived back at the shed, he saw a soaked Dad, Eamon and Maggie on their way in the door. Eamon and Maggie went straight to Peg, their faces a mixture of relief and concern. On seeing her masters, Peg gently and wearily wagged her tail.

'Aren't you a clever girl?' said Maggie, her eyes

filling with tears.

'That she is,' said Eamon, gently patting Peg's head. 'You preferred somewhere dark and quiet to have your family, didn't you, my girl?'

'Ok, everyone,' said Mam, 'Peg doesn't need a crowd of people.'

'We'll check the lambing shed,' said Dad, dragging Eamon with him.

Peter handed the supplies to his mother. He sat next to Peg and placed Shep's blanket on his lap, creating a pillow. Peg sniffed it and to Peter's delight, rested her head there. Mam covered the area under Peg and her pups with the clean towels.

With Kate and Maggie holding torches and Peter keeping Peg calm, Mam glanced over each pup and made sure they were able to suckle from their mother. Peg was still panting heavily. Moving her tail, Mam could see why. 'Here comes number four,' she announced.

As if waiting for the introduction, Peg lifted her head and hunched back as another pup entered the world. It was larger than the others.

'You are a big boy,' said Mam, working quickly to

remove the excess mucus before passing the pup to Peg to clean.

From her scan, Mam knew there were five pups to deliver. As they waited for signs of another, Mam checked the temperature of the four and weighed them before placing them back to suckle. Maggie jotted all the information down and placed a coloured band on each pup's paw so she knew which was which.

Looking at the thermometer's readings, Mam shook her head. 'This area is not warm enough. Peter, call Dad and tell him to get the battery-powered heat lamps from the shed.'

'Hot-water bottles!' exclaimed Maggie. 'I must have bought a hundred over the years, getting used to the cold weather in Ireland.'

Peter called Dad while Maggie went home to find every hot-water bottle she ever owned. She boiled water on the gas hob and filled them, wrapping each in a tea towel, then headed back to the shed.

At the same time, Eamon arrived with two heat lamps. As Maggie placed the hot-water bottles around Peg and her puppies, Eamon set up the lamps. He noticed Shep's blanket on Peter's knee. *What a good heart that boy has*, he thought.

There was still no sign of the fifth pup. 'Do think she's finished?' Kate asked Mam.

By now, Peg was exhausted, and with four hungry little pups, could she cope with another?

'Maybe the scan was wrong, Marian,' Eamon said hopefully. He was looking around for materials to fix the door so Peg and her pups would be warm for the night.

But Mam wasn't wrong, and she knew this as she placed her hand on Peg's tummy. It was time. Peg humped over and gave a small grunt before flopping back down. Mam gently eased the precious bundle from below Peg. It was a girl, tiny and not moving.

'It's so little,' whispered Kate, the light from her torch wobbling.

'Hold that torch still, Kate,' said Mam, as she gently removed the part of the sac the pup had been born in. She made sure nothing was blocking its tiny mouth and nose.

Peg's maternal instinct told her something was wrong. She tried to reach back to tend to her little pup, but with four others latched on and feeding, she couldn't move around.

With its nose and mouth clear, Mam felt along the pup's chest and realised it wasn't breathing. Seeing Mam's face, Maggie put a hand to her mouth. 'Oh no,' she whispered.

Eamon's face was ashen.

Kate's hand wobbled again as she struggled to hold the torch.

Peter closed his eyes, unable to watch.

Placing the pup in her left hand, Mam used her right hand to rub along its little back with a forward motion. Then she pressed gently on its chest and breathed into the pup's mouth. She continued this as the others looked on, hoping and praying for movement.

'Come on, little one,' Mam said in between breaths.

Suddenly the tiniest of whimpers could be heard. The pup's little body began to move up and down as its lungs filled with air and life. In one swift move, Mam placed the weakened pup at her mother's head.

'Go on, Peg,' Mam urged, 'you know what to do.'

Peg began to lick and nuzzle her newest baby,

cleaning the pup's tiny face and stimulating it to life. As Peg licked, Mam noticed the unusual markings on this little one: three black paws, and one that was white with black speckles. Now where had she seen those before …

Peg's licks worked their magic, and the little whimpers became a piercing cry. It was the best sound in the world. Nudging along with her nose, Peg guided the little pup as it crawled and stumbled to its brothers and sister. Soon all five, with eyes shut tight, were lined up enjoying their first family meal.

'Come on,' said Mam. 'It's time we left them alone.'

'You did so good, Peg,' whispered Peter, kissing the top of her head.

As they left the new family in peace, Kate and Peter met Dad coming back from the yard with a small bale of hay. He placed the bale in front of the shed door, blocking off any wind or rain that might try and make its way in.

* * *

The farmhouse was still in darkness as they entered. Mam boiled some water for tea and heated milk for hot chocolate. They all sat around the table, sipping their warm drinks in the cosy torchlight.

'Five little tails, twenty little legs,' gushed Maggie. 'Three boys and two girls, although the little one at the end gave me quite a fright.'

'My Peg is a natural protector,' said Eamon, beaming with pride. 'She never lost a sheep, nor a hen, and I knew she wouldn't let any harm come to her young.'

He lifted his cup of tea. 'Thank you, Marian and David, and Peter and Kate,' he said, as the others raised their cups too. 'We are truly blessed to have such good friends.'

'Did you notice the markings on the last pup?' Mam asked, taking a sip of tea. 'I know I have seen those before.'

'Three black paws and one white, speckled one,' remembered Peter.

'Hey,' said Eamon, sitting up suddenly, 'Mattie Kennedy's dog, Benji, has those markings.'

Peter looked at Eamon and then at Mam. 'Does that mean Benji is the daddy of Peg's pups?' he asked.

Mam smiled as she remembered the day she

caught Benji in her driveway. He must have been visiting Cooper's Farm too, and no one realised!

'They'll be the best-bred pups around,' gushed Eamon. 'But how are we going to tell Mattie Kennedy?'

'*We?*' laughed Dad. 'I think we'll leave that one to *you.*'

* * *

Over in the shed, it was cosy and warm. Five sleeping pups lay tucked in by Peg's side, their bellies rounded and full. Unable to keep her own eyes open, Peg too drifted asleep. So very tired, but so very content.

Chapter 7

Cakes Don't Bark

The next morning dawned bright and calm. Storm debris littered the roads, as workmen cleared branches and fallen trees, while engineers climbed poles to fix electricity wires. Peter and Kate's school was without power, so it would be closed for the day. On hearing this news, they had jumped in the air, giving each other a high five. No school and new puppies, BEST DAY EVER!

Over in the shed, Peg and her pups were sleeping soundly. Mam, Eamon, Peter and Kate peeked in from behind the door.

'We'll move them tomorrow, if that's ok with you?' said Eamon. 'Peg is still so very tired.'

'Look at the little one,' Peter said, pointing at the fifth pup, who was lying happily sprawled across her brothers and sister.

'She's a fighter, that one,' said Eamon, laughing. 'I'd say she's got great potential to be a top working dog.'

'Will you keep her?' asked Kate. 'Peg could train her in.'

'No, all those pups will be placed in new homes. Peg and Benji are the top dogs in the area, so no doubt we'll have plenty of interest when people find out the breeding.'

'Maybe we could buy her,' said Peter, looking to his mother. 'She was born here after all. It's already her home, really.'

'Oh yes!' said Kate. 'Please Mam, please, please, *please.*'

Mam shook her head. 'Absolutely not,' she said firmly. 'We have enough to do around here without having to train a new pup.'

Just then, Maggie arrived armed with supplies and freshly filled hot-water bottles. 'Come on, you two. You can help me feed Peg and check her bed. And as for you' – she turned to Eamon – 'it's time you visited a certain neighbour to tell him all about his dog's new puppies.'

Eamon's face fell.

'I'll come with you,' laughed Mam, and she and Eamon headed off in the direction of Mattie Kennedy's house.

Kate and Peter helped Maggie bring water and food to Peg. The puppies remained close to their mother.

'These little ones won't be able to see or hear for another while,' said Maggie. 'That's why they'll stay close to Peg, and she will be very protective of them.'

'Why is Peg still licking them?' asked Kate. 'Surely they're clean enough.'

'Little puppies need their mamas for many weeks and for many things,' Maggie explained. 'She is licking them now to help with their wee's and poo's.'

Peter's horrified face made Maggie laugh. 'You better get used to it!' she said between chuckles. 'There will be many puppy puddles and poos in our future.'

* * *

Two weeks after their arrival, Peg's pups were bright-eyed and full of mischief, making plenty of work for their humans. They were now happily settled into their new home at Cooper's Cottage, having left the shed when they were just two days old.

Peter and Kate adored the pups. Kate even opened a special 'Kate's Puppy Playschool', with chew toys, balls and teddy bears.

'It's important the puppies have time to play and develop,' she explained. 'I've been reading all about it in my library book.'

The pups rumbled and tumbled and chewed each other's ears, their little growls more adorable than terrifying. The youngest one – the one that had given them all such a fright on that stormy night – was by far the liveliest of the litter.

'Look,' exclaimed Peter, pointing at her, 'she has one blue eye!'

'Isn't it wonderful?' said Maggie. 'It's not unheard of for a collie to have a blue eye, but it is rare.'

As Peter gave her a cuddle, the little pup chewed on his collar. 'I'm going to call you Blue,' he whispered, 'and pretend you belong to me.'

On the same day that Blue got her name, Hettie the hen officially moved into her new home at Hazel

Tree Farm. Once Peg and her pups were out of the bike shed, Dad and Eamon had fixed the door and built a little roost for Hettie to sit on, as well as a nesting box to lay eggs. Kate was so excited at the thought of having fresh eggs for her breakfast.

'Not yet, Kate,' warned Maggie. 'Hettie is only eight weeks old. It will be a few more weeks before we see any eggs.'

It was such an exciting time for the children. Every day after their homework they went straight over to Maggie's, who always had brown bread and jam waiting for them. The children spent as much time as they could with Peg's pups, changing the newspaper when they did their wee's and poo's, and helping to line up their dinner bowls when they no longer needed Peg's milk.

When Peter and Kate returned home in the evening, the question was always the same: 'Pleeeeease can we keep one?'

But every time, their parents' answer was No.

'A puppy is too much responsibility right now,' said Mam. 'I just know after a week I'd end up having to walk it and feed it.'

'When the time is right, we'll get ourselves a new work dog,' said Dad. 'For now, we can share Peg with Eamon and Maggie, and that'll work out perfectly fine.'

Some days when their puppy work was over and Kate was busy playing with Hettie, Peter would call to see Blue again. By now she recognised her name, pricking her ears whenever she heard Peter say it. She had been so frail on the night she was born, but now she was first to the feed dish and first to inspect the new toys that Kate brought. She was brave, she was smart … but she wasn't Peter's.

Eamon and Maggie worried that Peter was getting too attached, and that heartbreak might be on the way.

* * *

Peg was a wonderful mother, and come May, her eight-week-old pups were strong and curious and up to all sorts of mischief. On sunny mornings, Peg would take her little family for walks around the farm, proudly showing them off to the sheep and hens.

She gave little barks to any pup that strayed too far

from her – usually Blue, the cheekiest one. She often ran ahead or trailed behind because a butterfly or leaf distracted her. She was far more interested in finding her own adventures than keeping in line.

At the lambing sheds, Eamon and Dad were hard at work mucking out the pens. Lambing season was over, and like Peg, the ewes were outdoors with their new babies, grazing on the fresh, sweet grass.

Eamon paused his work to watch Peg as she and the pups strutted by, Blue taking a moment to chase her tail.

That little one has a great sense of adventure, he thought to himself.

He knew this little pup would miss her brothers and sister when they went to their new homes, but no doubt Peg could do with a break. She was a devoted mother, but the rough play of her pups was starting to wear her out. Eamon was sure she'd be keen to get back to work – and glad to be the centre of attention at Cooper's Cottage once again.

As it turned out, finding four of the pups' new homes had been easy, and in many ways, it was thanks to Mattie Kennedy. The trip to his house the day after the pups were born had been tense at first. Even with Mam by his side, Eamon hadn't managed to fully convince Mattie how fine a dog Peg was and that the pups were so special.

'I'll be the judge of that,' Mattie had snapped.

This made Eamon cross. He wouldn't have anyone speak ill of his Peg, not after what she had been through.

Mam calmed both men down and invited Mattie to tea that night to see the pups for himself. He arrived in a new shirt, with combed hair and a pack of digestive biscuits, but the same scowl darkened his face.

But once he saw the puppies and heard the story of their arrival, Mattie Kennedy changed. His face lightened, and his mood brightened. In fact, by the time the second pot of tea was drawn, Eamon Cooper and Mattie Kennedy were sharing dog stories and picking potential new homes for 'their' pups.

'They can't go to just anyone,' warned Eamon.

'No, they cannot,' said Mattie, horrified at the mere thought.

'In fact,' said Eamon, 'you should pick a pup for yourself, Mattie.'

'Really?' said Mattie, tears in his eyes. 'I would like that very much.'

'No better teacher than your Benji,' added Eamon.

Mattie chose pup four, the large male, who he said had the same eyes as his Benji. Mattie left Hazel Tree Farm that evening with three slices of apple tart and a promise from Maggie that fresh brown bread would be on his doorstep every Friday morning. But he also left with a full heart, and that felt wonderful.

'Have you had any luck in finding the fifth one a home?' Dad asked Eamon now, as if reading his thoughts. The two men leaned on their forks and watched Peg and her pups, glad of the break.

Eamon shook his head sadly. 'Anyway,' he said, 'I often believe a dog chooses its own home, not the other way round.'

As the words left his mouth, Blue scurried away from her family once again and made a beeline for Hazel Tree farmhouse. A sharp bark from Peg brought her back, although not before Blue gave a cheeky little bark of her own.

'See what I mean?' said Eamon with a glint in his eye.

* * *

By the end of May, the puppies were twelve weeks old and ready to go to their forever homes. A delighted Mattie came to collect his pup, whom he was calling Billy. He rang later that day to say that Benji wasn't sure at first about this new arrival, and he growled whenever Billy got too close. However, things did improve and now father and son were happily curled up together on the sofa, snoozing.

From Peter's bedroom, the children watched as cars pulled up outside Cooper's Cottage and excited families jumped out, eager to meet and cuddle their new dogs.

Soon all the pups were gone, bar one. Blue, to the children's relief, was still without her forever home. However, a phone call a few days later was about to change everything.

Ring ring, ring ring, ring ring

At Cooper's Farm, Maggie answered the phone.

'Hello there,' she said cheerfully. 'What can I do for you?'

Nodding her head, she listened to the caller and a smile ran across her face.

'Of course,' she said. 'I'll have the little one all ready to go.'

* * *

It had been a long week in school, and the children were glad it was Friday. Kate went out to visit Hettie, happy that she still had her little feathery friend as her furry ones were finding new homes.

Peter headed next door to see Peg and Blue. As he arrived, he noticed that Maggie was clearing away the puppy pen as Peg lay snoozing in front of the stove. Blue was nibbling on her mother's ear. She jumped up when she saw Peter, who scooped down and cuddled her.

'That little one is off to her forever home today,' said Maggie as she cut some brown bread. 'Isn't that great news?'

But Peter couldn't answer. A huge lump swelled in his throat, and he couldn't get the words out. He just nodded his head and held in the tears as best he could. He looked down at Blue's little face, her twinkling eyes staring straight back at him.

With little interest, he nibbled on some bread and

jam. He placed Blue down, and without looking back, he trudged home, feeling miserable.

Kate and Hettie were in the yard beside the back door. Hettie was picking at a lettuce leaf that Kate had brought her.

'Peter,' exclaimed Kate, seeing her brother's face, 'what's the matter?'

'Blue.' Peter's words were choked in tears. 'Blue's going today.'

The children knew this day would come, but their hearts were still broken.

'There you are,' said Mam as they trudged in the door with faces as long as a wet weekend. 'Peter, I hope you haven't eaten too much bread and jam. Dinner will be ready soon, so go wash your hands after playing with the dogs.'

'Don't worry, because I won't be playing with them anymore,' Peter wailed.

'All the puppies are gone,' added Kate, standing at the back door, Hettie nestled under her arm.

'Oh,' said Mam, 'how marvellous they've all found a home.'

'It's not marvellous,' said Peter angrily, no longer

able to hold back the tears. 'It's the worst news ever.'

'Do you know the name of the new owners?' asked Mam.

Kate shrugged her shoulders.

'Will they even keep her name?' Peter asked, suddenly realising Blue might not be Blue anymore.

'What name?' said Mam. 'Ah, Peter, we said not to get too attached.'

With that, Peter burst into tears and ran into his mother's arms.

'Ah, love,' said Mam. 'We told you that when the time is right, we can have a dog of our own once again.'

But all Peter could think about was Blue.

* * *

That evening as they set the table for dinner, the children, especially Peter, were still feeling sad.

'Peter, concentrate,' scolded Mam as he overfilled a drinking glass, spilling water all over the table.

'Mmmmm, something smells good!' Dad called out cheerfully as he came in the back door.

'Hi, Dad,' came the unenthusiastic greetings of the

children, who continued to set the table.

Dad and Mam exchanged glances.

'Oh, I forgot to mention,' Dad said rather loudly, 'I invited Eamon and Maggie to dinner.'

'How lovely,' said Mam, grinning. 'You'd better add another two settings, Peter.'

Just then, there was a knock at the back door. Peter went to open it, Kate by his side, ready to greet their guests. But it was just a smiling Eamon.

'Where's Maggie?' asked Peter, looking behind him.

'She's on her way,' said Eamon. 'She's putting the finishing touches to her Trinidad sponge cake.'

In the distance, the children could see Maggie walking towards them, holding a small, square box and grinning from ear to ear.

'I'm coming!' she called out. 'I'm coming.'

By the time she reached the door, her face was flushed and she was quite out of breath.

'Here,' she said, giving Peter the white box. 'You take this and make sure you put it somewhere safe.'

'That's a very special Trinidad sponge,' said Eamon. 'We wouldn't want anything to happen to it.'

'Why is this cake so special?' asked Kate.

Taking the box, Peter started to walk to the kitchen table. He had only taken a couple of steps when something in the box moved, he was sure of it. Do sponge cakes move?

'Everything ok?' asked Mam.

'I think so,' Peter stammered as he looked down at the two large flaps that loosely covered the top.

Suddenly the box gave a little bark. Cakes don't bark! This was a bark the children knew only too well.

'BLUE!!' cried Peter as he put the box on the ground.

A little nose pushed its way up through the flaps, and on seeing Peter, Blue bounded against the side of the box, making it fall over. She rolled out onto the kitchen floor before scrambling back up and running into a sea of hugs and cuddles from an ecstatic Peter. He covered his face in her soft fur and huge, wet licks.

'It's Blue, it's Blue!' squealed Kate.

'Is she ours? Is she really ours?' begged Peter, as Blue licked and nipped his chin.

'Yes,' said Dad, laughing. 'She really is.'

'I told you she was going to her forever home

today,' smiled Maggie. 'I just couldn't quite remember where that was.'

Dad pulled a little collar out of his pocket. A silver circle hung from it, with Dad's phone number etched on one side and the other side blank. 'We can get this engraved with her name,' he said, showing it to Peter.

'By all accounts, she seems to know her name,' laughed Eamon. 'Blue, is it?'

'Meanwhile, I picked these up earlier today,' said Mam, taking two shiny dog bowls out of the press, which was also crammed with tins of puppy food and treats.

'You two proved how ready you are to own a dog,' added Dad. 'You helped Maggie every day with feeding and minding the puppies, and we came to understand how special this little one is to you.'

'There could be no better home than right here,' added Eamon. 'Although little Blue had already picked her owners, if you ask me.'

Peter wasted no time in filling Blue's dishes with food and water.

'Not too much,' said Maggie. 'Remember she only has a small tummy.'

Soon the whole family, along with Maggie and Eamon, were sitting down to dinner.

'To friends old and new,' said Dad, raising his glass of orange squash.

'And to new beginnings,' added Mam.

'Cheers!' The children's beakers clinked and splashed.

'Phew, so many new arrivals,' said Eamon. 'Lambs, chicks and puppies, sure it's nothing but new beginnings and new life here at Hazel Tree Farm.'

* * *

Before heading to bed that night, Kate checked on Hettie. She was perched on her roost, her head tucked under her wing. Kate quietly put her hand into the nesting box, feeling around the straw and hoping that there might be … She gasped. Still warm, an egg sat proudly on the golden straw.

'Well done, Hettie!' whispered Kate, taking the egg and rushing indoors to show the others.

As they headed to bed, Peter and Kate could not remember a time when they were so happy.

Peter giggled as he tried to smuggle Blue into his

bedroom. 'Stop wiggling! They'll see you,' he whispered.

'You're going to get into trouble,' said Kate.

'It's only for tonight,' said Peter. 'I promise.'

When they were safely inside his room, he pulled a pillow from his bed. 'This is for you, Blue. You can sleep on this tonight.'

Blue began to chew on the corner of the pillow and then tugged at it with all her might.

Meanwhile Kate was dreaming about how she was going to cook Hettie's first egg the next morning.

'Peter,' she called across the hall, 'isn't it exciting having Blue and Hettie?'

'The best,' replied Peter, as he stroked Blue's tiny belly. 'What adventures we will have.'

Blue wrapped her paws around his hand and tried to chew playfully on his fingers. Her little tail wagged and her eyes, one blue and one brown, twinkled up at him.

''Night, Peter,' said Kate.

''Night, Kate,' said Peter.

Yap, yap, said Blue.

Join Peter and Kate, Blue and Hettie –
now all a year older – for more adventures in
Blue the Brave, the next book in the Hazel Tree
Farm series. Read on for a short extract ...

Find out more at obrien.ie/hazel-tree-farm

By the side of Peter's bed, Blue dozed, happily trapped in that magical moment between dream and awake. She yawned and stretched, lifting her back leg to gently scratch her ear. As she did so, she could have sworn she heard a low growling noise carried along by the breeze. She pricked her ears and sat bolt upright.

The outside winds were flowing into the room through the open window, bringing with them the secrets of the night.

Blue's nose tingled. She caught the faintest whiff of something strange. It was not a familiar scent … and it was definitely not a friendly one.

She ran to the windowsill, jumping up and resting her front paws on it. She leaned her head and nose out the window and let out two muffled barks, just loud enough to wake her sleeping master.

'Blue,' groaned Peter, 'stop it, you'll wake everyone up.'

But Blue was not concerned about waking her humans. Her senses were telling her that something dangerous was out there, and she needed to get out and get out – fast.

In the henhouse, Rodney the rooster puffed out his feathers and lifted his wings. The hens were in danger, and they were all trapped, with nowhere to run and no one to help them. Puffing out his chest for all he was worth, he did the one and only thing he could do … Call for help.

COCKADOOODLE DOOOOOO000000oooooooo! he crowed with all his might.

COCKADOOODLE DOOOOOO000000oooooooo

COCKADOOODLE DOOOOOO000000oooooooo!

He caused great alarm in the henhouses, and the rest of the hens began to cluck and squawk too.

Back in the house, Blue was also alarmed. On hearing Rodney's crows, she didn't need another warning. There was a trespasser – the animals were under threat. Yelping and barking, she scraped at the bedroom door. She had to get out, she had to help the animals.

Peter jumped up and threw on his clothes. He knew his dog sensed something, but he didn't want Blue to wake his parents up. They already didn't like her sleeping in his room, and if she woke them up, that would be it for sure.

He threw open his bedroom door and Blue dashed out, nearly flattening poor Kate, who was sleepily wandering back from the bathroom.

'Shhhhhh!' Peter whispered, before Kate could scream and cause even more commotion. 'Blue senses something outside, and I can hear noises coming from the Coopers' henhouse. I'm going to check it out.'

'Hettie,' mouthed Kate in alarm.

The little hen had not come when Kate called her earlier. Mam had told her not to worry, that hens enjoy being outdoors as the weather picks up. 'She'll find her own way home, you'll see,' Mam had said. 'We'll leave the shed door open so she can put herself to bed tonight.'

But Kate had a bad feeling, and now a deep dread and panic came over her.

'I'm coming too,' she whispered in a frantic tone. Running back to her room, she threw on some clothes and met her brother and Blue in the kitchen.

By now Blue was frantic. She was scratching at the back door, her nails leaving marks. She looked at her masters, begging them to let her out.

Grabbing a torch, Peter fumbled with the door key as Kate tried to keep Blue quiet.

CLICK!

The noise of the lock opening was almost deafening in the stillness of the house. The children looked at each other in panic – if their parents weren't awake by now, that would surely do it. They paused, but they couldn't hear any sounds from upstairs.

'Phew.' Peter let out a sigh of relief.

He opened the door. Blue burst out and ran towards the gap in the hedge that led to the Coopers' yard and the henhouse.

'Come on,' said Kate, her voice trembling. 'We'd better go too.'

Out they ran after Blue, into the dark night, slamming the door behind them.

LÁ DOMHANDA
NA LEABHAR
WORLD
**BOOK
DAY**
2 MÁRTA 2023

Happy
World Book Day!

When you've read this book, you can keep the fun going by: swapping it, talking about it with a friend, or reading it again!

What do you want to read next? Whether it's **comics**, **audiobooks**, **recipe books** or **non-fiction,** you can visit your school, local library or nearest bookshop for your next read – someone will always be happy to help.

LÁ DOMHANDA NA LEABHAR

WORLD **BOOK DAY**

2 MÁRTA 2023

World Book Day is about changing lives through reading

When children **choose to read** in their spare time it makes them

| Feel happier | Better at reading | More successful |

Help the children in your lives **make the choice to read** by:

1. **Reading to them**
2. **Having books at home**
3. **Letting them choose what they want to read**
4. **Helping them choose what they want to read**
5. **Making time for reading**
6. **Making reading fun!**

SPONSORED BY

NATIONAL **BOOK** tokens

Changing lives through a love of books and reading

World Book Day® is a charity sponsored by National Book Tokens

Illustration Allen Fatimaharan